DEAD BODIES BITE

BOOK ONE

Dead Bodies Bite

John Del Toro

Published by Trellis Publishing, 2021.

This is a work of fiction. Similarities to real people, places, or events are entirely coincidental.

DEAD BODIES BITE

First edition. July 12, 2021.

Copyright © 2021 John Del Toro.

ISBN: 979-8224981564

Written by John Del Toro.

JOHN DEL TORO

1

DEAD AGAIN by ROBERT GATTO

"Sir, I need to speak with you urgently."

Doctor Zachary Jones straightened up from his microscope, rubbing his eyes and the back of his neck. He'd been working for the past fourteen hours without a break, with only a steady supply of coffee to keep him going. He was torn between being irritated at the interruption and relieved at the excuse to stop for a moment. His lab was silent, only the occasional distant scream could be heard echoing through the facility.

"What's up Mike?"

"The coroner from Zone 3 just couriered over a toxicology report from a recent murder victim, I think you should take a look at it."

Zach looked surprised at the statement. "He couldn't use email?"

Mike shook his head. "Signal's down again and the power's unstable. You're running on the backup generators but the rest of us are struggling with an intermittent supply again. God knows what the status is over in Zone 3. They're probably out altogether."

"I don't know if God has much to do with it anymore," Zach replied wryly. "I think we're on our own now."

Mike shrugged. "We're doing our best to rebuild things, but there just isn't enough people left to maintain everything, and not enough experts left for troubleshooting. We're still broadcasting the announcements over the air waves asking people to come, telling them we're offering employment, food and a place to stay, but nobody new has shown up for months. Contact with the scouting parties is obviously sketchy at best, but last we heard, they'd covered another seven states and hadn't found another living soul. It's looking like we gathered everyone up first time around."

"Dammit, we can't be the only people left in the whole of the United States! There's barely a thousand of us in each zone, that's less than six thousand people. With my contact with other bunkers before we lost them, I would estimate that the survivors at the time were in the region of thirty thousand at most. Last year, the population was three hundred and twenty *million*, and that was the ones that were registered and accounted for."

Mike sat down. "I know, it's crazy, the whole thing was a total shit storm, but right now, I need you look at this report."

"What's so special that a coroner can't handle his own murder case," Zach muttered, holding his hand out for the document. "It's not as if there's a lot of suspects left to choose from."

"I'd go straight to the toxicology report and look at the blood analysis if I were you," Mike advised.

Zach flipped the pages and finding the appropriate section, settled down to read. Ten minutes of silence ensued before Zach looked up with a panicked expression on his face.

"It can't be," he said helplessly.

"I was hoping I was wrong,"

It was the only answer Mike could give under the circumstances.

"Believe me, I'd have been happier to be interrupted for nothing, I can't believe this. I thought we'd wiped them out, apart from the ones we've got under lock and key."

To emphasize his point, another inhuman scream echoed through the underground facility where the public health department headquarters was now situated.

"You're absolutely certain that this is the same strain?"

"No doubt, but just in case we're acting like a couple of hysterical teenage girls, let's compare the print outs and double check."

After five minutes of silence while the two compared the reports, Zach stood. "We have to admit it, he was bitten or scratched by a zombie, he's infected with exactly the same strain of the virus that caused the first outbreak."

"That means there's still one out there, and we've led everyone to believe the streets are safe now."

"Not necessarily," Zach replied. "Is there any chance he's connected with research, that he would have been handling one of the captives for some reason? Maybe he just got careless."

"Afraid not, he was scanned completely clean before being dispatched to Zone 3, he's been working at the power plant ever since, trying to keep the grid up and running. That's where he was last seen."

"I hope everyone who handled the body stuck to procedure, else we've got another outbreak on our hands. Do you know if it's been incinerated yet?"

"The report doesn't say."

"Well for God's sake, find out, and make sure everyone who came into contact with this guy is thoroughly scanned. It's bad enough that there's still at least one running about out there, the last thing we need is the virus to be already on the inside."

"What are you going to do Zach?"

Zach sighed deeply. "First, I'm going to read this full report so I'm up on all the facts, after that, I've no idea."

Chapter Two

Zach maneuvered the motorbike through the city streets, carefully navigating what would have been a normal and noisy traffic jam but was now eerily silent and still. He'd decided that if he wanted a job done properly, he might as well do it himself. He was heading for Zone 3, but progress was slow. The cleanup operation that had been in place for months now were doing a good job of returning the city to a habitable state, but after the last of the zombies had been hunted down, all the remaining people found and scanned for the virus, they had been concentrating on removing bodies and incinerating them. Once that gruesome task was over, they'd begun on rubbish and rotting food, a huge problem since everyone's lives had been so suddenly and dramatically interrupted by the apocalypse that had hit them.

Half-eaten meals were left on tables, crawling with maggots and flies, fridges and freezers with no power were now filled with oozing mush which bore no resemblance to the groceries they'd once been, garbage cans and dumpsters crawled with rats and other vermin, omitting toxic stenches that polluted the very air around them. Zach shuddered to think of the stores and hypermarkets that had been filled with fresh produce. Yep, the cleanup crews had their work cut out for them, and they were making some pretty impressive headway, but they had more immediate worries than the graveyard of abandoned cars, trucks, vans and other vehicles that littered the roads, the result of the panic which had caused everyone to try and flee the city, hoping the virus was contained to one area and they could escape their fate.

Zach had initially hoped the same thing, but as a member of a government funded research team, he had been one of the first to hear that it was happening in every state countrywide, and spreading at a rate that no amount of forces could contain. The resulting loss of human life had been a greater tragedy than he could ever hope to express with mere words. He had gathered as much Intel as he could before lines of communication went down and it was every man for himself, isolated in their own small area. He and his team were aware of something most Americans were not, that every major city held at least one secure underground facility designed to protect the President in the event of terrorist attacks or natural disasters, wherever he may be at the time of their occurrence. Zach and his team had made their way there, with as much equipment as they could safely carry, moving rapidly under the cover of darkness and gathering up as many survivors as they could along the way. They sent out daily hunting parties, both to kill the zombies and to rescue as many of the human race as they could find uninfected. The bunker was designed to withstand anything anyone could possible imagine, and was stocked for the survival of hundreds for many years. Zach had immediately set up a broadcast over the airwaves giving detailed directions to safety. He also had the hunting parties place signs all over the city, begging people to come.

At first, people had arrived steadily. The bunker was spacious and equipped to outlast even nuclear radiation, but it had never been designed for so many. They had food and water, a state of the art medical facility and research lab, an extensive library, but what they lacked most severely was space. Living conditions became cramped and uncomfortable, so they had made plans to wipe out the threat and reclaim their society. They'd been through hardship and trauma, but through it, they had grown stronger. Some were already natural warriors, eager to unite and fight a common enemy, while others had to learn to ignore the horror and devastation they faced, overcoming their fears for the survival of the race. Zach was proud of each and every one. Slowly but surely, they had wiped out the zombies, taken the lives of those infected but not yet turned, and taken control of the city, gradually trying to return it to its former glory and reinstate all the systems that had been in place before the collapse of everything. Before communications went down, Zach had made contact with nine other bunkers across the country. They were occupied mostly by high level military personnel who had access codes, as many of their own teams that had survived, and rag tag bunches of survivors, just like Zach's own bunker. They had between them, coordinated a sweep of the USA with military precision, and had been in the midst of it when they lost contact. Only when Zach had completed his own instructions had he felt it safe for the people to return to life above ground, splitting the city into six manageable zones and allowing the people to choose their employment and place of residence.

Zach had worked tirelessly ever since, studying the virus, even requesting live samples of the creatures which were held in secure cages in the underground facility, in order to study them and to draw samples of blood and tissue to work with. He still had no idea where the virus had originated from, but his main purpose was to try and find a cure. Watching a loved one scream and beg for his life after being scanned positive for the virus, and having to ignore their pleas and end it for them before they could turn and infect others, was possibly the hardest thing to deal with throughout this horror. He was determined to put a stop to that, to find a cure that could halt the virus in its tracks and preserve the precious lives of the remaining few. His ultimate goal was one that could reverse it even after the infected had completely turned, but he'd settle for the first for now. Suddenly, he came across the sign that announced he was about to enter Zone 3, and he was surprised to find that he'd been lost in thought the whole journey. Concentrating now on the road, he headed for the crematorium which had been commandeered by the coroner to act as his new morgue, allowing for easy disposal of infected bodies. Nothing could be allowed to hang about for long these days.

Two guards stopped him at the door and he was required to remove his helmet and present some identification, only then was he allowed to pass. The coroner and the newly appointed chief of police were deep in conversation when he entered the room. Neither of them seemed surprised to see him. Zach didn't bother wasting time with pleasantries.

"Has the body been disposed of?"

"Of course," the coroner replied, shocked that he would be considered so incompetent as to not follow basic protocol.

"Good. Now gather up everyone, and I mean absolutely everyone, who had any contact with it at all, however minor."

"They've all been tested Zach," Pete, the chief of police told him gently.

"Yeah well, the virus can take a while to incubate and show itself. I'm testing them again."

"As you wish," Pete sighed, leaving to give the order.

"Might as well start with you Jimmy," Zach said, as he removed a pack of needles and a bulky handheld machine from his inside pocket. Reaching into the other side of his leather biker jacket, he removed a pack of gloves, a mask, a pair of goggles, and a batch of medical slides. He laid his equipment out on the desk and advanced on the coroner. Jimmy looked fearful as he rolled up his sleeve and presented his arm as Zach donned the safety equipment. He'd seen the gun strapped to Zach's hip as he'd pulled his jacket open, and he knew Zach wouldn't hesitate.

"I followed all the procedures," he whined as Zach drew a small amount of blood from his vein.

"Then you'll have nothing to worry about, will you?"

Zach proceeded to place a small drop of the blood on the slide, covered it with a sliver of membrane, and slid it into the machine. He pressed a few buttons then headed over to the bright yellow and black box marked for incineration and dropped the needle in. He returned and perched one hip on the edge of the desk, waiting for the machine to start throwing numbers at him. He had studied the virus extensively, he knew exactly the elevations and drops to look for to indicate that it was beginning to take hold, to slowly incubate, hiding in plain sight within its victim.

Jimmy was visibly sweating by the time Zach turned to him. "You're clean."

Jimmy sighed deeply with relief and swiped at his brow. "I'm the one who had most contact, I think testing the others is a waste of time and resources."

"Yeah, but the others might not have followed protocol as strictly as you. Look, Jim, we've got the same situation as we always had, people now concentrated again in the cities. You know how fast this happens, one infected person could wipe out all of Zone 3 in a matter of days or even hours, and you can bet your ass they'd move across the city searching for more food. The last thing you need is someone on the inside turning."

"I know, I know, it's better to be safe than sorry. It's just that they're all good men, I know each of them personally and I guess ... well, surviving this has created a bond ..."

Zach's expression softened. "I understand, I feel the same way, but until I can find a cure ..."

He left the rest of the words unspoken as the others began to enter the room. All of them were visibly relieved as they all tested clear of the virus that turned good men into drooling, slavering, mindless creatures that hungered for human flesh. They shuffled out of the room, no exuberance in their reprieve, only a thankfulness that left them almost weak with gratitude. Only Pete and Jimmy remained with Zach.

"Okay, so now that's over with, let's review this. The report said that the actual cause of death was a gunshot wound?"

"Yes, not an immediate kill shot, but he would have bled out within minutes," Pete replied.

"And nobody's coming forward to admit to the shooting?"

"We've questioned everybody and nobody seems to have any knowledge of it, and I believe 'em. The vic, Tom Smith, was last seen leaving the power plant at the end of his shift with his payment in food as usual. Reports all say he was same as ever, no weird moods, no unusual plans. He was found next morning by the Area West cleanup crew, who reported immediately. Location was on his way home but there was no sign of his food bag."

"So what's your theory?"

"Guess we got ourselves a lone drifter, who probably shot him for the food. We've been hunting but haven't managed to find him so he's probably moved on. I'm sending out an alert this morning to all areas to be on their guard and advise people not to carry food in plain sight."

"What about the bites?"

"There were only two, which is unusual, so my guess is that the creature was right there, getting in quick before Tom actually died. We know they don't eat dead flesh so I reckon it got the two bites in before he passed, then left him alone after that. I was hoping you could tell us why he didn't turn."

"Probably because he was so close to death and bleeding out," Zach shrugged. "The virus didn't have time to take hold and there wasn't enough blood still moving through the system to carry it."

"That makes sense," Jimmy interjected. "I had the same thoughts myself. I'm sorry he's dead but I'm glad he didn't turn into one of them."

"And you've found no sign of the creature either?"

"Nope, not a trace," Pete confirmed.

"Do you think it's possible the drifter and the zombie are one in the same? That maybe he was carrying the virus and turned just after the shooting?" Jimmy asked.

Zach considered the possibility. "It'd be one heck of a coincidence, but we know the virus takes about 48 hours to incubate fully and change the entire body, but when it does, it's almost instant. I guess it might be possible, he'd have been feeling pretty sick by then, maybe making him desperate enough to kill for food, putting his illness down to malnutrition or even starvation. But I'm not the only research facility with live samples, any reports of anybody losing one?"

"I sent people out to ask the very same question," Pete said. "So far, the ones that have come back have given a negative."

The three men digested the information in silence before Jimmy summed it up. "So either we've got a newly turned creature, or we've got one hell of a smart-assed zombie who's hiding out until opportunities arise."

"Either way, it's gotta be stopped or we'll have a second outbreak on our hands, and if it's one of our own guys, it'll retain some base memories of which areas of the city are active, and maybe even where the underground shelter is."

"Dear God, what are you gonna do, Zach."

"I'm gonna do what has to be done. Go out there and hunt the bastard down."

Chapter Three

Dressed as he was in head to toe black, biker leathers, from his heavy, buckled boots to his tight gloves, Zach looked more like a character from an action movie than the research scientist he was. The image was helped along with two guns at his side, held there by the holsters crossed over low on his hips. Another was concealed beneath his biker jacket in a shoulder holster and a long-range rifle was slung over his shoulder. In addition, his pockets bulged with ammo, and several knives were secured about his person.

"Are you still sure you want to do this alone? It wouldn't take more than a few hours to gather up and kit out a hunting party from all Zones. The military boys would handle this much better."

"We might not have hours, it's knocking off time soon and people are going to be on the streets heading home. This needs to be done now."

"At least let me come with you, it should be my job."

"Listen Pete, I know you mean well and I know you think you're better equipped for the job, and you're probably right, but if we're right in thinking this thing is deliberately hiding out and waiting for opportunities, then it's showing more intelligence than any of the others. Being alone might just offer it the opportunity it needs."

"So you're setting yourself up as bait?"

"If it comes to that, then yes, but hopefully I'll be bait that bites back."

"Just make sure you bite first."

Zach looked at Pete with a serious expression. "If I fail, I can rely on you to do the right thing?"

Pete returned his steady gaze. "I'd advise you keep the helmet on at all times, but if you get bitten or scratched, just make sure you take it off before you turn so we have a clear and clean head shot."

"Understood."

The men shook as they parted, each wondering if they would ever see the other again. Once out on the street, Zach checked his watch. The power plant was the largest place of employment in Zone 3 and there would be a shift change soon, he intended to be there, watching and following people home. They'd all been advised to travel in groups and carry weapons at all times, but there were always some that wouldn't heed the advice. If the thing was going to show itself, he wanted to be there to meet it.

He slid his leg over the bike, negotiating the panniers that had been added. One was filled with extra ammo for all his weapons, the other contained fresh water, a few energy bars and a walkie talkie in case he needed assistance out on the road. He could have done without the food, he could survive longer without it than the zombie would take to find another victim. If he began to starve before he had killed it, it would be all over for them anyway. The bike gave a powerful roar as he shot off into the growing dusk to head to the power plant.

Zach sat and watched from the shadows as people began to spill from the plant, talking and joshing each other as people who closely work together every day tend to do. It gave Zach a pang of sadness, it felt like a distant memory from a past life, something safe, something normal. At first, the people stuck to various groups as instructed, not quite as alert to their surroundings as Zach would have hoped, but at least heeding some of the warning. Zach followed on foot, and as the groups split to head in different directions, he tried to decide which one to stick with. He assessed them quickly. One group contained a guy that was on the outskirts, hanging back and not joining in the general conversation. Making his decision, Zach jogged back for the bike.

He'd quickly made it back and sure enough, the guy had split, walking off on his own down another street. Zach had figured him for a loner and as such, he'd probably picked a building to live in that didn't have any other occupants. He couldn't blame the guy, they'd all thought they were safe. Zach parked up the bike again and followed on foot, keeping to the shadows. He was relieved and disappointed when the guy made it safely to a large apartment building with no incident. The outer door was locked, and Zach caught a glimpse of the heavy steel reinforcement on the inside as the man unlocked it then swung it open and darted inside. He heard several locks and deadbolts click into place behind the man.

The loner was home safe, but Zach couldn't give up on the nagging feeling that he wouldn't be the only one to think he was the best chance for a zombie dinner. He decided to take a wander around the neighbourhood and see what he could throw up. With no real clue as to where to start, it seemed as good as any other. With the streets completely devoid of human life, Zach found himself with nothing to do but think as he walked and watched.

He had figured out a lot about the virus, but still didn't really understand it. The body seemed to be dead, the heart no longer beat, the organs didn't function, the flesh itself was dead, feeling no hot or cold, no pain, no injury too great to ignore completely. Yet they weren't dead in the sense we normally understood. To create that desire, that need for flesh, that never ending, driving hunger, synapses in the brain had to be firing. It was this that brought around the rudimentary intelligence, the memory patterns and the social interaction. He had watched them closely in captivity. They recognized their own new, strange species, accepted one another and even formed close bonds with some around them. They were protective of each other, and when given food, it might look like a horrendous, violent frenzy but if you looked closer, there was order to it and it was ensured that everyone got a partial share of what was available. As he'd watched, Zach had determined that more and more of the brain had seemed to fire up again over time, the sparks of certain areas kick starting others. Their intelligence increased the longer they survived. His main question now was whether the body would rot and fail before they regained full intelligence. If it didn't, even the ones in captivity posed a serious risk and would have to be destroyed, cutting Zach off from his research material.

He wasn't sure what he was dealing with here, but it seemed unlikely to be an older zombie, it had attacked the dying man too quickly. That seemed to imply one fairly recently formed, which meant to go undetected as it had, it had retained much more of the thinking process. Zach was pulled from his inner musings by a rustling noise from behind a set of dumpsters up ahead. He walked forward with more caution. If it was from inside, it was most likely rats. The vermin had survived and thrived on the rot and decay left behind by the people ripped from their daily lives. As he approached, he determined that the noise was coming from behind the bins, not inside.

He pulled one of the guns from the holster, releasing the safety and chambering a bullet, readying the gun to fire. He crept forward as quietly as he could in his heavy boots and flipped his visor down, protecting his eyes from possible infected blood spray or grasping, gouging fingers. He ducked down as he reached the bins, using them as cover as he slid along the front and round the side. He paused there, steadying his breathing and preparing himself for what he might find. With one final exhale, he turned the corner, gun raised, finger poised on the trigger.

A stray dog looked up at him and snarled, head low, a deep, menacing growl forming in its throat. It advanced one step, protecting whatever disgusting meal it had found. Zach almost laughed with relief but didn't want to be forced to shoot the dog if he caused it to attack. Other than the vermin and bugs that bred at rapid rates, animals were a scarce commodity in this new world. One day, this half-starved mutt might once again be someone's companion, their comfort in a lonely existence. He stepped away, allowing the animal to grab its prize and scarper.

He had surmised from his research and information that the virus didn't seem to effect any other species of life, although test subjects had been hard to come by. There were no reports or any zombie animals among the cities and those few he had captured to inject directly with infected blood had shown no ill effects and after a few months of observation, he had been able to release them with no concerns about the safety of the survivors. Similar reports from more rural areas with a wider range of species had confirmed their suspicions that it was only humans that turned. However, animals did seem to suffice as a meal for the zombies when they couldn't get to human flesh, but Zach had yet to fully understand their need to eat, since it didn't seem to sustain them in any way. It was just another piece of the puzzle, and hopefully, he would stay alive to solve it. His relieved reaction to the first tense moment had reminded him just how ill-equipped he was for his current task, his only advantage his basic understanding of the creatures he had been studying.

Chapter Four

Throughout the night, Zach searched, covering what he could working in an ever increasing circle out from the power plant, still certain that the concentration of people and the constant presence of human flesh was what had drawn the creature into Zone 3. He used the bike to cruise the streets, then would return to likely looking buildings to hunt through them. Despite his importance as a research scientist, he had not excluded himself from the original hunting parties so was not without some acquired skills, but every time he entered a building, he felt like a young boy poking a hornet's nest, aware of the danger he was stirring up but too intent on his purpose to stop.

As dawn rose, the only thing of interest he'd found was a recent camp, the empty food tins scattered around letting him know it belonged to a human, possibly the drifter that had shot Tom Smith. That was one for the police chief, he would report it later, if and when more pressing matters were resolved. Feeling the need to relieve himself after his long night, he headed to one of the many abandoned service stations. He wasn't sure which buildings had a water supply in Zone 3, so best to use a public urinal rather than a bathroom in a private residence and be unable to flush, the city had enough problems.

He entered cautiously, stepping over the fallen shelves and scattered goods that remained, mostly motor oils and cleaning products for cars that no longer ran or couldn't be negotiated through the blocked up streets and highways even if they did have some fuel left in the tank. Shattered glass and spilled produce littered the floor, evidence of the panicked raids that had taken place in the early days, and he crunched his way across them, aware he was making too much noise but unable to find a clear path to the back where the restroom was located. He stopped halfway, pausing to see if his presence had attracted any attention. Silence.

He moved on and pushed open the restroom door. It groaned on hinges stiff from lack of use and Zach entered. The small corridor was pitch black as the door swung closed behind him and he scrambled for his flashlight, sighing in relief as the beam showed the corridor still empty. Locating the door to the men's room, he was more prepared, removing one of his guns and readying it. With both hands occupied, he pushed the door open with his shoulder, almost expecting a screaming, snarling face to appear the moment it opened. He had created the image so clearly in his mind he was almost surprised when nothing happened. The room itself had high windows which provided natural light from the rising sun so he clicked off his flashlight and tucked it safely back into his pocket. One by one, he checked the stalls, not wishing to be taken by surprise while he was otherwise occupied. The room was clear.

Zach was relieved to step back outside, buildings held no sense of safety or security any more. Instead, they provided too many places to hide, too many dark, shadowy areas where danger could lurk undetected or where you could end up cornered and trapped, the safe haven becoming a tomb. He gave an involuntary shiver, recalling the early days when screams of rage and terror, both human and inhuman, were all that could be heard from wherever you tried to hide. He was still incredulous that he and most of his team, all scientists focused on their research, distracted and not even equipped to live in the real world, had made it through this. He removed his helmet and retrieved a bottle of water from the pannier, leaning against the bike as he took a big swig, still contemplating his own dumb luck. He couldn't help but wonder if the survivors, himself included, had got too cocky, too confident of their success. Suddenly, from the corner of his eye, he thought he spotted movement.

Zach turned quickly and saw the figure of a male in the distance. The man too had stopped in his tracks on spotting Zach and for a second, they stared at one another. The figure was large, almost six foot tall, broad at the shoulders and from what Zach could make out, was dressed in army fatigues. As it didn't scream and make its way towards him, Zach figured it was somebody from the Zone out on a routine patrol, but the way he was staring made Zach nervous. He raised his hand in a wave of greeting and his movement broke the spell between them. Zach's water bottle fell from his hand as the man turned to run, and gave away the uneven, clumsy, loping gait of a zombie.

Zach immediately gave chase, cursing himself for having the rifle jammed along the side of the bike, unready to fire, and for all the guns having their safeties on. He had taken too many precautions and now they slowed him down as he fumbled with one of the hand guns as he ran. The creature had disappeared around a corner, and as Zach skidded round the same one, he came to a halt. The street was empty. He examined the buildings on either side, all apartment blocks by the looks of it. It could be inside waiting in any one. Zach took several steps down the street, careful to stick to the middle of the road. Up ahead, he could see a dead end, explaining why the road was devoid of abandoned vehicles, only a few parked cars sat at the side of the road in allocated parking bays. It had to have ducked inside a building on this street, the wall at the end was too high and smooth to scale. He gave himself time to wonder at the intelligence of that move. Perhaps he was mistaken? Maybe this was just a man surviving out here on his own. An injury could have caused the awkward gait and Zach hadn't really been close enough to tell one way or another.

"Hello," he called out. "Is anyone there? I'm not looking to hurt anyone, I'm hunting a creature, not a person."

Other than his voice echoing, there was no reply. It occurred to Zach that this person might be the drifter who'd shot and killed Tom Smith. If that was the case, Zach was a sitting duck out here. He didn't carry food, but his weapons and bike would certainly be worth killing for. He moved closer in towards the parked cars, hoping they would give some cover if anyone opened fire on him. He continued to move down the street, slowly, turning every few steps to ensure he kept an eye on every approach, glancing up at windows as he did so. He slowed as he came upon a car with the sidewalk side doors and trunk partially open.

He tried to peer into the car as he approached but his vision was obstructed by the sun glinting off the windshield. He reached the hood, sliding his way along the side of the car, both hands gripping the handle of the gun. He could see now that the front was empty and the back seats appeared that way too. Didn't mean to say someone wasn't hiding on the floor in the back. He move further forward, allowing himself a better view. The car was empty. He took a deep breath and steeled himself to check the trunk. Once again, an image filled his mind, a man hiding there, on his back, gun at the ready, Zach's face blown to smithereens by repeated shots the minute he stepped round and raised the trunk. He pushed it away and moved fast, intending to fire the first shot. His plan might have worked, but he was left staring at the bullet hole through the bottom of the empty trunk, the sound of his shot ringing in his ears, blocking out the sound of the door to his right opening. The next thing he knew, something slammed into him, sending him flying into the middle of the road where he stumbled and fell.

Chapter Five

Face down on the ground, Zach heard the inhuman, guttural scream and he scrambled to turn around to face his assailant. His leathers had saved him from any injury during the fall, but he'd lost his grip on the gun, which had skittered across the road out of his reach. He didn't have time to retrieve another as the creature was almost upon him. As Zach stared at the hollow, almost skeletal face, the dripping, slavering jaws and the tattered army clothing, he was left in no doubt what he was facing this time. He felt frozen, like a rabbit in headlights as it lumbered towards him, favoring its left leg.

Breaking his fear-induced paralysis, Zach bent both knees and waited, using every inch of his inner resolve not to attempt to get to his feet in the few nanoseconds he had before it reached him. Poised, he waited. As the creature reached and bent forward with its anxious maw, Zach kicked as hard as he could, landing his heavy boots dead center on the monster's chest, sending it staggering backwards, flailing its arms to keep its balance. Zach got up and advanced, the zombie meeting his attack head on, showing an inordinate amount of strength as they grappled, Zach attempting to bring the creature to its knees. The creature attempted to get at his face, the only exposed part of his body, his leathers protecting him from the long, ugly scratching talons and the snapping jaw as they fought and punched.

Finally, Zach managed to take advantage of the weaker leg, another hefty kick to the knee dropping the half man, half animal. Zach quickly applied the handcuffs provided to him by Pete before he set out, intending to retrieve them after the deed was done. The creature knelt there, head down, arms behind its back, silent, as if it already knew what fate awaited it. Zach stood in front of it as he removed the second handgun from his hip holster. The metallic snaps and clicks of him preparing the gun to fire echoed back from the empty buildings around them. He raised his arm, carefully aiming the gun at the bent head in front of him, taking his time in hopes of a quick, clean kill.

"Don't."

Zach stared, hardly able to believe what he thought he had just heard, his expression almost comically incredulous. "What? Did you just ... *say* something?"

"Please ... don't ...shoot."

The voice was hoarse and cracked, like an old man left abandoned in a neglectful nursing home that'd had no occasion to use it for many years, the words uncertain, hesitant. This was impossible! The basic level of brain activity that remained after the virus had wreaked its havoc was not enough for speech. He had seen some of the older ones communicate only with uncoordinated touches and basic grunts, and he'd had no reason to believe it would ever advance beyond this. Scientific curiosity overcame him, and he studied the creature more closely. Judging by the clothes and the state of the body, it wasn't old, had only turned a month or two ago at most, there was no way it should have regained this level of intelligence so fast. Despite feeling ridiculous, he spoke in return.

"Why shouldn't I?"

The creature raised its head and Zach gasped. Yes, the hollow face and dripping jaws screamed monster, but the eyes! They weren't the usual empty, staring voids of nothingness he'd come to expect. They were dark brown, and in them, he could read emotions, anger, sorrow, despair, he saw them all flicker within. Slowly, the gun began to drop.

"Help me," it pleaded, the words barely formed around the swollen, blackish tongue.

"What are you?" Zach asked, more to himself than anyone else, not really expecting an answer.

"Infected."

Zach put his gun away and knelt down on the ground beside the creature. It shrank away.

"Too close, can't stop."

Zach backed up a little. "Are you telling me that you don't want to hurt me but you can't help yourself? That the urge is to strong."

The creature nodded and turned it's large, dark eyes upon him, pleading and longing at the same time.

"Do you remember how you were infected?"

"Remember ... everything."

Dear God! Zach struggled to get his head around the possibility, how it would feel to remember everything about you that was human and right, yet be trapped inside a body that craved to rip and tear at human flesh, the urges too great to ignore. This man was in a special kind of hell and part of Zach told him to put the thing out of its misery, but the scientist in him couldn't listen. This was something different. For some reason, the virus hadn't eradicated the man inside, and he needed to know why.

"Listen to me, I can try to help you, but you need to help me. I need to take you back to my lab. I need to study you, your brain, your blood, your tissue. I'm trying to find a cure, will you come back with me?"

"Bite."

"Yeah, okay, I get it. You'll bite me at any opportunity. Guess the bike's out of the question then."

Zach looked around, wondering what to do. He wished he'd decided to carry the walkie talkie with him and not leave it with the bike, but he hadn't really anticipated a use for it other than if he needed to report in for a team to come and kill him before he turned. There was no one in sight that could help, and even if there were, he would be reluctant to enlist their services. They would want to kill this thing in front of him straight away, seeing only one of the abominations that had almost wiped out civilization, not understanding the importance it might have. His team were the only ones who could be trusted. Zach had no choice but to get back to the bike and retrieve the walkie talkie. He turned to the kneeling zombie.

"Wait here, I'll be back in a sec."

With no reason to believe the creature would obey, Zach sprinted back to where he had left the bike. He grabbed the radio and turned it on, calling back to Zone 3 base and putting in a request for them to get Mike to contact him on a certain frequency. He left the radio on, its volume turned to high, and slipped it inside his top pocket. Spotting his motorcycle helmet sitting on the seat where he had left it, he snatched it up before racing back to the spot he had left the zombie. To his great relief, it was still there, kneeling in the middle of the road. Zach rushed up behind it, slamming the full-faced helmet on over its head and buckling it tightly under the chin. It didn't even try to fight and seemed to gladly accept Zach's help to get to its feet. With its mouth covered and hands still cuffed behind its back, Zach began the long walk back to Zone 1, hoping the call from Mike would come soon. Just because the creature was docile right now didn't mean it would remain that way. Perhaps the human side was in charge right now, and that could shift at any moment. As unprecedented as this way, there was no way to tell. He'd already had a taste of how strong it was, if it chose to fight, he'd given it a weapon and protection by putting the helmet on.

They'd been walking for about thirty minutes when the radio sparked to life inside his pocket. He paused, letting go of the hold he had on the cuff chain to answer it.

"Mike, I'm at the crossroads of," Zach glanced around, looking for street signs. "Jefferson Avenue and Lincoln Drive. Can you plot a route to get a car through to pick me up? I've got a live one I need to bring in."

"Sure," the voice crackled on the other end. "I'll get the army boys out to you."

"No, no army, not this time. You know they hate me keeping the things alive. Any resistance and they'll shoot to kill, and I really need this one."

"Fine, but it might take me a while to get to you. I don't know the roads like those boys."

"That's okay, we'll head along Jefferson and keep moving west, just find us as soon as possible."

"Will do. Be careful."

Zach tucked the radio away and carried on walking. An hour later, he'd never been more relieved to hear the sound of an engine in his life.

Chapter Six

The journey passed without incident, except for Mike's pure disbelief at what Zach had found. Unwilling to make the back seat passenger act like a performing monkey, he'd refrained from conversing with it just to prove himself right for Mike's benefit. He would see soon enough. As they pulled up as close to the entrance of the underground facility as they could, Zach wondered if he should have blindfolded the creature as an extra precaution, just in case it should escape. Figuring he was too late, the two men went ahead with the transfer.

Suddenly, the thing decided it'd had enough and both were thankful for not only the motorcycle helmet they'd left in place, but also the army personal who heard the guttural screams from below and came running to assist. It took four of them and the scientists to get the enraged zombie into a cell and sedated.

"This one should be eradicated immediately, it's too strong," the one in charge declared, glowering at Zach.

"It's caged now, its fine. Thanks for your help, we can take it from here."

With one last uncertain look, the military personnel left the two men alone with the zombie. Zach had taken the precaution of placing it alone, unsure of how the others would react to it. He was afraid they would recognize it as different from them and attack it.

"There's no way that thing spoke to you, you must have been hallucinating. Lack of sleep, dehydration..."

"I know what it looks like, Mike, but how do you think I managed to get it restrained and the helmet on if it didn't let me? You've seen how strong he is."

"Oh, so it's a he now? Zach, you're losing the plot."

"Just please trust me and help me out here. The army personnel are already making noises about not keeping him, that he's too strong to be safe. If they get any inkling as to how intelligent it is, I won't be able to reason with them. Stay with him, and when he comes round, tell him to keep it hidden except from you and me, okay?"

"Sure, I'll sit and chat with the flesh eating zombie, no problem."

Mike was disgruntled and still disbelieving, but Zach knew he'd come around once he saw what he'd seen, and he knew he'd do as he'd been asked. Secure in the knowledge that his new acquisition was safe for the moment, he headed into his lab with the blood he had drawn from him once the sedation had taken effect. Putting a drop on a slide, he inserted into the same type of machine he's used and left behind at Zone 3 the day before. He waited impatiently for the results to collate, then watched in amazement as for the first time the machine let him down. The read out on the display screen was going haywire, unable to settle on any figures, the numbers changing every few seconds until they became such a blur, Zach could no longer read them.

"Must be faulty," he muttered, whishing he hadn't left the other one behind.

He placed another drop of blood on a fresh slide and slid it under his microscope. Focusing the delicate piece of equipment, he couldn't quite believe what he was seeing. On the slide, a war was raging. Healthy, human cells were under attack from ones already affected by the virus, but just as fast, the normal cells were fighting back, almost eradicating the virus completely before being overcome once again. The man's entire bloodstream must be a mass of constantly changing and adapting cells.

"No wonder the machine went nuts!" Zach murmured, his thoughts already racing as to how to identify what this man's blood contained that allowed it to fight the infection. If he could pinpoint it and enhance it, he was not only well on the way to finding a cure, but he could also create a vaccine for immunity against the virus. As long as he had a supply of this man's blood long enough to figure it all out, he could ensure the survival of the human race and prevent this ever happening again.

Jubilant, he dashed from the lab, hardly able to contain himself, desperate to share the news with Mike and get him working on it with him straight away. He didn't pause when he heard the half-human scream echoing in the corridors, he was used to that. When the following rally of gunshots rang out in response, Zach stopped in his tracks. Mike came down the corridor with an apologetic look on his face, a deep scratch down his left cheek.

"I'm sorry," Mike said. "I'm so sorry. He spoke to me Zach, he actually spoke! Intelligent conversation. My God! I couldn't believe it. I let my guard down, Zach, I got too close. I've let you down."

An armed army officer stepped round the corner, his weapon aimed at Mike. He spoke into a radio clipped to his shirt. "Subject one neutralized, subject two in my sights."

Zach dropped to his knees and sobbed.

END

OUR DEAD BODIES by Jerry Wright

The ax felt heavier in his hand than it did when he chopped wood every autumn for the winter. He knew the weight was emotional and not physical but there was still something contradictory about the ease with which it arced over his shoulder and closed the distance to the teenager's head. She didn't have a great deal of hair left, and he wondered briefly if that had anything to do with how effortlessly it seemed to cleave her skull. She crumpled to the ground in front of him. The ax didn't travel with her but her body simply slid off in a sadly anticlimactic way. He had to sidestep because his grip had loosened and the ace head swung down and toward him.

She was dead and—

Could he call her that? If the unnaturalists were right, she died weeks or even months ago. Hell, if the unnaturalists were right, the immediate guilt and self-loathing that washed over him was inappropriate and wasted emotion. He felt it, though.

She couldn't have been older than fifteen when she was... alive? He didn't quite buy the theory that the girl hadn't been alive before the ace fell. If not death, then what? Trauma, yes. Resurrection, maybe. Some kind of resurrection unlike everything promised. There was no glorious new body, no virgins, no cavorting with the gods. There was only an ace that cleaved too easily and belied the significance of the end.

He didn't know if she lived before the ace fell or if she was dead. In any case, that part of her life in which she was rational couldn't have lasted for more than fifteen years. Perhaps that part of her life ended months ago, perhaps as long as a year ago. Every part of her life was over now.

He leaned against the ace, resting the head on the ground. He wanted to wipe the blade on the grass but he couldn't come up with the energy, couldn't come up with any energy at all. She wasn't bleeding. That part of the whole mess was the most disturbing. . Somehow, the fact that blood didn't seep from her and pool around her made everything seem hopeless along with violent. It made the loathing seem contradictory as well but that didn't mitigate it at all. It seemed wrong, and he wished he could somehow make the death more visibly significant, less like killing a prop

A sudden rustling in the trees to the left of the campsite startled him and the ace instantly came back up as he whirled toward the noise. Two men stepped forward.

Men, alive in every sense.

They held shotguns, and when they saw him, the guns lowered. "You got her for us, then," one said amicably.

He let the ace return to the ground and sighed. "You were hunting her?"

"Yes," the man replied. He was short, ruddy faced, and wearing camouflage he'd probably bought from an army surplus store years before everything went to hell. The companion was thin and mousey. Images of the old cartoon with the big bulldog and the tiny terrier leaping around it in sycophantic bliss came to mind and he resisted the urge to make a comment. "Good thing you knew how to take care of business. I guess we drove her this direction." The man smiled and rolled his eyes. He shook his head and lifted his hands almost apologetically. "Her? Hell. It." He stepped forward slightly and said, "Green. Donovan Green." The man nodded to the other. "That's Sean Arcineaux."

"Hal North. Lot of them out here?" Hal was true. North was not.

"Not anymore. We patrol these parts for Spring Kettle. You from Spring Kettle?" Hal shook his head and Green continued. "Little town about eight miles down the road. About two-thousand survivors." *Survivors.* The world was mostly survivors, and towns like Spring Kettle probably only had a dozen or so to address in the first place. Hal nodded anyway and hoped he seemed impressed, raising an eyebrow slightly.

Green seemed happy. He seemed ecstatic. Hal wondered how many hours he'd prepared for the job with an energy drink in one hand and a video game console controller in the other. Green finally found his calling and Hal wondered if he were proud because it had only taken a tragedy of biblical proportions. He sighed again and nodded toward the girl's body but Green asked, "Where you from?"

"Dallas." He wasn't from Dallas. He knew, though, that Dallas had suffered more than any other city so that some neighborhoods lay in ruins. "Not sure where I'll go next."

"Spring's not a bad place."

"I'm going to head north. Got family in South Dakota." Another lie. He expounded on it. "No idea if they're still alive."

Green nodded. "Yeah. They ruined everything." It wasn't true. Humanity did. "You okay here? We only saw signs of this one but there could be more around."

"I'll be okay. My car has a full tank. I think I'll just pack up and head North."

"We'll burn the body. Otherwise it'll attract others."

Hal nodded. "I have some lighter fluid in the car."

"One day all of these fucking zombies will be dead," Green said.

Hal winced. He hated the word. Green's expression changed and Hal shook his head and said, "They destroyed everything. Hope that day comes soon."

Green nodded. "And life can go back to normal." Hal was pretty sure nothing on Earth would make Green unhappier. He didn't answer but went to the back of his car, opened the trunk, and pulled out the bottle of fluid. He saw his shogun in there and picked it up, too, pumping a round into the chamber. He paused and closed his trunk just as Green cried out, "Jesus! Look out! There are two in your car!"

Hal felt the familiar sickness crash over him as he brought the shotgun up and fired. Green's head exploded in red mist. Arcineaux screamed but Hal's second shot brought him down. Hal walked over to Green and looked down sadly on him. Most of his head was gone. This time, there was plenty of blood.

He stared at Green's body for a long time and wondered why he'd been more troubled after killing the teenager than now. He was still troubled but there was no guilt, no loathing. He turned around and opened the car door. "It's okay, Honey," he said. "You and Kaylee can come out now."

***

"We'll leave them," he said. "We just don't have time."

He waited as she nodded, an excruciatingly slow process now though the comprehension showed in her eyes immediately. He'd spent the first months fighting the urge to finish sentences or otherwise hurry the conversation along.

They weren't rotting. Not yet. Maybe they wouldn't. There were theories abounding about all of that. Of course, the unnaturalists wouldn't hear about it. To them, they would rot because they were dead and their bodies were unnatural. Others, those who held to the virus theory no matter how many times it was debunked, portrayed it all as mind over matter, as the minds convinced the bodies they were dead. Others, primarily those who debunked the virus theory, claimed it was a mutated version of leprosy, and the rotting occurred at an accelerated rate simply because of the inability to feel pain and thus address small wounds. Somehow, the bacteria caused encephalitis in some and not in others, so some became violent and some didn't.

Hal thought that last theory the most likely but it didn't account for the sudden outbreak in various geographical regions. The lack of pain was real, though. He'd seen Kaylee slice the palm of her hand on a jagged piece of metal, seen her keep playing with no indication she felt any pain at all. He'd scrubbed the wound and bound it and then taken a book on leprosy from the library, wistfully wishing the government, which undertook heroic efforts to keep certain institutions in place, would have done the same for libraries. Knowledge would certainly be lost in a generation unless the growing anarchy somehow slowed.

The books stressed something called visual surveillance of extremities, VSE, as a means to prevent rot. Evidently, the key to living with leprosy was scanning your fingers and toes constantly and by doing so catch any small cuts for treatment before they became infected. Of course, Kaylee and Lori couldn't do it themselves. That meant he had to constantly survey their extremities. It was habit now, Hal guessed, as they removed themselves from the car and helped him pack up the campsite.

They were still them.

He saw it less and less lately but they were there beneath whatever dullness the condition brought. They were there behind the strange, pinkish pupils that revealed their condition to Green and Arcineaux. They were there, and so far outside of their eyes their bodies still seemed like them. He knew they were there. Mannerisms remained that proved it, the way Lori inclined her head and sighed when Kaylee frustrated her even if the phrase "Young lady, don't make me ask again" had shortened to "Young lady, don't" in a long, low sentence that took three times as long as the original. Kaylee still climbed in his lap to say, "Please, Daddy!" even if the journey took her a minute or two and the words were barely recognizable.

The unnaturalists were winning.

They were winning and it was open season on the infected, which Hal guessed made a lot of sense to some. The violent infected behaved just like the movies, not moving like the creatures with that weird shuffle but still killing and some even eating their victims. The unnaturalists were winning but there was no distinguishing between the violent infected and those who weren't.

Hal took the bodies of the two men and placed them with the teenage girl. She'd been violent, beyond hope. At least, she'd been beyond help. He took their weapons along with their ammunition and put it all in the trunk, returning with the lighter fluid and dousing their bodies. Between the two of them, Kaylee and Lori had managed to pull the tent's spikes out of the ground. He sighed, squirted some lighter fluid on a twig, and lit it with his lighter. He dropped the makeshift match onto the bodies and, satisfied with the minor inferno that resulted, walked to help with the camp. He let them work on the tent and instead packed up the little stove and the mesh grill for the campfire. Those, too, he put in the trunk.

He considered letting them finish the tent. Even though she couldn't communicate it, he knew Lori felt bitterly disappointed when he had to help her with a simple task. He grew too worried about it, though, too concerned others would come for Green and Arcineaux. He walked to the tent and put his hand on Lori's arm. "Honey. Let me do the tent. Can you and Kaylee throw sticks and branches on the bodies?" Lori nodded, her pink pupils seemed to dilate for a moment, and then she turned and walked to Kaylee. She moved slowly, more slowly than she had before. Still, it wasn't at all like the lumbering monsters from the movies. He watched her for a moment.

She was still beautiful.

She was still beautiful and he hadn't touched her for six months.

He'd wanted to. Of course he'd wanted to. They'd been active, very active, prior to Hell descending to Earth or rising up on Earth or however the damned metaphor worked. They'd gone at it like rabbits for the first year of their marriage and still went at it for most of the pregnancy. Lori became aggressive only a few months after Kaylee was born, and they'd been rabbits again. Nine years they'd been rabbits. Now they didn't do a thing, and he didn't know if he was supposed to do something or if she would or if it hurt her or if she'd be hurt by it.

He was pretty sure she wanted it. Even with all the changes, he could sometimes catch a wistful expression on her face, the one that replaced the almost placid kind of blankness that seemed to characterize their outward emotions if not their inward. He wondered if he should just do it. They would have no trouble finding an abandoned hotel on the road and there ought to be one with adjoining rooms. He could get Kaylee occupied and just do it. She felt unattractive to him plenty of times before all this. Perhaps that was the issue. Perhaps she thought he didn't want her. He could sleep with her to reassure her.

Yeah. Of course that could all be rationalization.

When the car was packed, he used the rest of the lighter fluid to make sure the bodies and branches would keep burning. Despite all of the predictions, things weren't too hard to come by. There had been some hoarding in the beginning but when people realized not enough of society had been destroyed to upend everything, the hoarding slowed down. Production had slowed for everything, stopped for most things. Really, though, that only meant there weren't a lot of pre-packaged snack chips. Vegetables and meat were still plentiful, sold mostly from little stands rather than giant mega stores.

Why did he do that? Why did he do everything he could to pretend the end of the world hadn't come? Why did he do so much justification? *Sure, everything got blown the fuck back to the Old West but hey, all the movies acted like we'd be back in the Stone Age.* There wasn't a lot of comfort with it but it helped him keep up the hatred for the people who would kill Kaylee and Lori, the people who walked around like road warriors in a world that, if anything, had plenty of gas and water left.

"Medicine." It took Lori almost ten seconds to say the word, and though he understood what she wanted he waited until she was finished and then nodded. He wondered if it made a difference to her, him not jumping ahead but waiting. He opened the bag in the trunk and pulled out three pills for each of them. Rifampicin was a leprosy drug. He'd taken it from an abandoned pharmacy. They didn't have the other two drugs used to treat it but he knew they were all antibiotics. The other pills were just antibiotics. He had bottles full of different varieties that all ended with *cyllin*. If it all really did come down to bacteria, maybe it was helping.

Lori swallowed the pills and then made Kaylee swallow hers. Hal closed the trunk. "We should get on the road now, Honey," he said. She nodded and got Kaylee settled. It was inefficient. Hal could have strapped in her much faster but he believed Lori needed it. When she finished, Lori closed the car door and began her slow walk to the other side. "Would you like to ride up front? If we see a car, you'll have to pretend you're sleeping."

She smiled. At least, he thought she smiled. There definitely seemed to be at least a small upturn in the corners of her mouth. He intercepted her on the way to the door and pulled her to him, holding her tightly. He felt her arms tighten on him as well and had to fight back tears. He pulled back slightly and kissed her forehead. "I love you," he whispered.

He held her through the minute or so it took her to say that she loved him too.

***

The road was lonely. It felt strange to know they would likely drive for hours without seeing another car even though humanity hadn't become devastated into little pockets of survivors like all the films. People tended to stay close, though, tended to treat everywhere outside of their particular environment as wilderness. He glanced at the gas tank. They had a quarter tank, and the dashboard told him that was good for another hundred and seventeen miles. Gas wasn't much of a problem. There were still gas stations working in the larger cities and still pipelines and refineries keeping it going. Demand had dropped dramatically, though, and he filled his tank far more often from an abandoned vehicle than at a pump.

He glanced at Lori. She sat with her eyes closed and he wondered if she did that just to make sure her limited ability to react quickly wouldn't lead to their discovery. She rarely slept anymore, perhaps an hour or two per night. He looked at the rear view mirror. Kaylee's pink eyes stared forward. She noticed him looking and took an eternity to smile. He smiled back and scanned the horizon for a place to stop. Dusk, almost.

The mountains had already given way to a long stretch of plains, the kind of Southwest stretch that meant tiny towns that abruptly changed the speed limit from seventy-five miles per hour to thirty-five. Most of those towns were empty now, citizens more comfortable in heavier pockets of population, citizens more comfortable with authorities killing the infected so they didn't have to. As though the highway itself heard him, a sign came up, advertising Honey Blossom Rock as forty-two miles away. "Ready to stop for the night, Kaylee?" he asked.

It took a long time for her to get out a reply, and it took him a moment to realize she was asking him for ice cream when they got there. He hoped there was some left in one of the stores. He said, "We'll see," and then slowed because there was a semi-truck on the side of the road up ahead. It looked like it might be from the seventies and he thought that meant there was a chance for gas rather than diesel. He could take diesel, use it for lighting fires or something along those lines but it wouldn't fuel the car. He pulled beside it and Lori wasn't sleeping because her eyes opened when the car stopped. "I'm going to see if I can fill the tank," he said.

She managed to say, "Okay," and this time it was difficult to hide his impatience because in this new world—*Brave New World*, he thought bitterly—stopping in an unfamiliar place was dangerous. He held back, though, and remained in his seat until she finished and then opened his door and stepped out. He grabbed the six foot length of rubber tubing he used for transferring fuel and started walking toward the tractor to find the gas tank. He tried but failed to keep from looking at the trailer itself with its art. A family sitting down to dinner. The paint was faded but he could see the bright and smiling face of the mother holding a roasted chicken, could see the indulgent father and the boy and girl looking hungry. Alford Meats. Making families smile since 1974.

He wondered if there was food in the back of the truck but dismissed the idea. He couldn't hear the refrigeration unit working, if the truck even had one. It was possible the truck had been abandoned here years ago anyway. The gas would be old but it would work. He made his way forward and found the tank. It was enormous, a hundred or maybe two hundred gallons in a long silverfish cylinder that seemed to be placed too close to the hitch. He found the cap and held his breath as he wiped grime from it. He sighed. Diesel fuel only. He dropped the hose onto the ground and stepped to the cab to see if anything else could be scavenged.

The roar reached him before the impact but it didn't give him a chance to avoid the attack. He was able to avoid resistance so the momentum carried him away, stumbling, from the infected man.

Woman.

He turned around and backed away as she approached. If she'd been the driver of the truck, she was about as stereotypical a female truck driver as they came. He could see through years of grime the remnants of a flannel shirt of some kind. It was stained, along with what was left of her jeans, with blood, some of it fresh. She roared again and started toward him and he realized he'd stupidly left his weapons in the car. There was no easy way to get them because the truck driver stood between Hal and the weapons. She was long dead if dead was an accurate description. Portions of her skull were visible along the side of her face and the sickly white of her jawbone stood in horrible contrast to the strangely intact gums and teeth and tongue.

She was beyond hope. He could see that. Already her eyes glinted with excitement, instinct for violence. He scanned for something, anything. Realistically, his only hope was evasion but it wasn't a false hope. Though the sick didn't really lose any of their physical speed, they lost a great deal of their dexterity, their reaction time. He dove to the ground and rolled beneath the truck. His aim was off and he felt a sickening and sharp burst of agony as something caught on his shirt and dug into his flesh before tearing away as he rolled over. He gained some time, though. The driver let out a gurgling scream and he kept rolling until he'd rolled through to the other side. He was on his feet and moving before the creature decided how to follow. He paused for only a moment before heading toward the rear of the trailer. Nine times out of ten, someone as far gone as the lady would eventually decide to run in the shortest route but the idea of crawling under the truck would be difficult for her to manage. Around the trailer would get him to the weapons while she probably still waited.

So, when she slammed into him, sending him sprawling over the sand abutment and rolling into the overgrown drainage ditch, it took a moment for him to understand what the hell had happened. He felt slickness on his face and retched as he lifted himself up and tried to understand the situation. He'd rolled into gore, rotting intestines or rotting meat or rotting something. He wiped his eyes with the back of his hand. Coyote. There was a partially eaten coyote carcass, probably the truck driver's dinner for the last few days. He retched again and then felt her again, this time wrapping her arms around him as she attacked. He rolled, primarily to get her beneath him rather than above, and then he lifted his upper body up and slammed it backward.

Of course, it was no use.

There was no pain. Or, at least, the pain was dulled so damned dramatically that there was no pain enough to shock a zombie—goddam, he hated that word—into letting go. He tried again, this time grabbing her wrists through the flannel and pulling them apart. That separated them, and he leapt up and stumbled a few feet away until he could jump over the abutment and back to the truck. He wanted to run for the car but at this point he wasn't certain he'd make it, certainly wouldn't be able to get to the weapons easily. What he needed, more than anything else, was a moment to breathe.

The cab.

He rushed to the passenger door and yanked. It was locked. He rushed around and yanked on the driver's door. It opened but as he tried to step up, he felt her arms on him again. He slammed outward with the door but it only made her slide down so she gripped his legs and he ended up holding onto the seat belt to keep from falling. These situations always left him with a curious sense of conflict. The woman was clearly beyond hope, beyond any help he could offer her. Still, he couldn't bear to think of her as anything other than a woman, as a woman who once had hopes and dreams and perhaps still did. How could he? If she were beyond hope than wasn't it just inevitable that Lori and Kaylee would be beyond hope soon?

Kaylee. Lori. Ultimately, the need to protect them overcame his hesitance and though he winced as he did it, he lifted his free leg and brought it down hard on the truck driver's shoulder. The woman grunted but didn't stop.

Woman.

Creature.

Thing.

He tried desperately to consider her a thing as he pulled his foot back and brought it down again, this time on her face. He got a gurgled scream from her but her hands still didn't relax their grip on his leg. If anything, her grip tightened and Hal felt something visceral and realized it was real fear. It was urgent fear, fear he'd lost some time ago in the omnipresent state of continual, frightened despair. He cursed himself for leaving his weapons in the car, cursed himself for an oversight that would surely kill him and more importantly leave Lori and Kaylee unprotected. He kicked her again but again it did nothing to loosen her grip. In fact, she screamed and yanked hard and he found his own grip failing and slid down the seat belt strap so that she was able to throw her arms around his waist.

Then he saw it. He cursed himself because he should have known it would be there. Didn't most truckers keep them? The butt was about a foot away but it was risky because to reach it he'd have to let go of the strap with at least one of his hands. Hell, the damned thing might not be loaded and all he'd have would be a club. He had to risk it, though, and he shouted to give himself some energy as he let go with one hand and grabbed for the gun. His hand closed around the stock beneath the trigger, and the truck driver finally won the tug of war so both of them fell backward. The gun came out with them but he couldn't keep a grip on it, and it tumbled to the left while he and the woman tumbled to the right. She lost her grip momentarily with the impact of the fall and he scrambled away but she grabbed his leg again before he could get clear.

The gun—he could see it was a shotgun now—was about three feet past his outstretched hands, and he clawed at the ground to try to close the distance. He made about six or seven inches of progress but she yanked him backward so he lost it again. He rolled over and a rock on the shoulder of the road bit into the small of his back so that he screamed as sharp pain shot through him. It angered him, and fueled by the anger he kicked out again with his free leg, catching the driver on her chin, a solid kick that sent her sprawling back. Of course, she leapt for him again but he'd gained the time he needed. When she landed on him, the shotgun was pointed at her. It ended up wedged against her midsection and he pulled the trigger.

And not a damned thing happened.

For a moment, nauseous fear gripped him. The damned thing hadn't been loaded after all but as the butt dug into his shoulder, he realized he'd never pumped the action, so he screamed again and grabbed the pump with his free hand, pulling it down and hearing a satisfying click. He still didn't know if it was loaded but he pulled the trigger. The explosion left him hurt and deaf. In the struggle, the butt of the gun had moved to his chest, and he felt like something broke from the recoil. The driver, though, flew back and landed on the ground, her midsection more like shredded rags of flesh than a body. She was screaming, Hal thought, but the sound of the gun still rang in his ears so he couldn't be sure. He got to his knees, and the movement sent shards of hurt from his chest. Bruised ribs maybe but broken ribs probably. He still had to deal with her.

Head shots always killed them. They weren't the only things that killed them but they always did the trick. He could feel a tear running down his cheek as he lifted the gun to his shoulder again. He aimed for her head and hesitated because he knew the recoil would hurt like hell. Finally, the sight of her screaming face was too much and he whispered, "I'm sorry," and pulled the trigger. The sound was distant but the pain in his side was profound, and he saw the woman's face disappear in red mist as the edges of his vision blackened. He felt the ground beneath him leap up and then felt hands on his cheeks.

He opened his eyes.

It was night. He'd been out for at least three hours. Lori held his face in her hands.

***

He watched the fire as it flickered, sending interesting shadows against the truck. It took a great deal of time but he learned from Lori he'd been out for an entire day. She'd managed, with Kaylee's help, to drive the car behind the truck. That, in and of itself was remarkable. She'd grazed the driver's side against the trailer so there was a wide gash but appearance didn't really matter anymore. She'd left him on the ground, afraid to move him, but she and Kaylee had scavenged the truck. She'd put everything she thought might be of use in a little pile. There was a first aid kit, flares, and some blankets. There were also cigarettes, and Hal smoked one now. None of the food in the trailer was good except for a case of teriyaki beef jerky. A few packages of it was boiling along with a few onions and some canned corn over the fire.

There was something both frightening and reassuring about her actions. He was pretty sure she wouldn't have been able to keep things together if he'd been dead. On the other hand, he wasn't entirely certain she knew he'd wake up. Still, she hadn't reacted with blind instinct. She'd reacted, against all odds, as the Lori before all the shit hit the fan. She'd reacted, and she and Kaylee weren't wandering the desert or declining. Kaylee slept in the car at the moment but she sat beside him, and Hal looked at her in wonder. "You did good, Lori," he said.

"Well," she said. It took a long time to get out, and he looked at her expectantly. She stared back at him and said, "Well." He waited. "Not." He still watched her, trying his best not to become impatient. "Good," she said.

It took him a moment, and then tears welled up in his eyes. Well, not good. She'd corrected his grammar. She'd corrected his grammar! He reached for her and pulled her close to him, and before he could think about it, his mouth found hers.

Six months, really closer to three quarters of a year. He felt like weeping the entire time but he didn't, and she hadn't lost any of her skill even if she'd lost some of the speed. It was slow, sweet. When he finished, he lay atop her and felt the warmth of the fire against his sides and kissed her and finally wept. She slid her hand slowly up his back until she found his head and she stroked his hair softly and kissed his neck and his cheek.

They woke in the morning and his chest felt better but Lori insisted, in her way, that they address the injury so he used a roll of cloth sports bandages to wrap his ribs tightly. When he was finished, they woke Kaylee and ate jerky stew for breakfast. Kaylee played quietly at the side of the truck as they packed the car, and when he closed the trunk, Lori said, "Thought...you...didn't...want...me...anymore." He felt tears threatening and pulled her to him.

"More than I ever have, Lori." He fought back the tears. "More than I ever have."

He held her until she let go of him and called to Kaylee. He found it interesting that the two of them had no trouble finishing each others sentences or more commonly simply reacting to what the other was attempting to say. Kaylee made her way over, and for a moment Hal didn't recognize the feeling he felt. It was hope.

He secured them in the car and turned the engine over. He backed up and saw a car in the distance behind them. "Get down," he said. They obeyed but he felt a horrible sense of foreboding anyway, and he realized the car was slowing down. "In the glove box, Lori," he whispered. He kept his eyes focused on the rear view mirror and waited until Lori pressed the gun into his hand. The car was slowing, only about twenty yards back. The headlights filled the car and he lifted up his hand to make sure they could see the gun in it.

The car slowed and then pulled up beside them. The man in the driver's seat appeared to be alone. He was Hal's age. Maybe a little older. A lot more sedentary. Probably an accountant or a middle manager before the shit hit the fan. He too held a gun. Hal pressed the button on his door to bring the window down and the man did the same with his passenger window. "I don't want any trouble," the man said. Hal didn't reply and the man said, "Any food left in the truck."

Something about the man's eyes seemed vaguely familiar. It wasn't just the fear because the fear was on everyone's face these days. There was furtiveness. He hid something. Hal brought his gun down but only so he could chamber a round discretely as he said, "No. Well, yes. There was only some beef jerky, a case of it. We only kept about half, and the rest is around the side of the trailer."

The man nodded. "Thank you. I'll drive around. I don't want trouble."

We. God damn it. *We only kept about half.* That was an inexcusable mistake but the man didn't seem to notice. He nodded again and moved his car forward and Hal sighed in relief but then saw movement in the man's backseat and lifted his gun. He thought for a moment he caught a glint of metal but then dropped his gun. It wasn't silvery or even reflected tail lights. The glint was pink. The infected ducked back down but the glint was pink. Hal realized he was shaking as the man pulled in front of the truck and turned his engine off.

Hal turned his engine off, too, took a deep breath and stepped from the car.

"Please!" the man said. "I don't want any trouble." Hal looked at the man. He stood with his gun pointed toward them but his stance was all wrong. He didn't know how to use it.

Hal lifted his hands up and said, "I'm not going to hurt you. I don't want trouble either. I just want to show you something. Please, put down the gun and come over here."

"You want me to get rid of my gun."

"No," Hal said. "You can bring it. Just stop pointing at me." The man seemed like he was lost for a moment and Hal added, "We can help each other, maybe. Please. I won't hurt you and I won't hurt whoever's in the car." It was the wrong thing to say, and the man's eyes grew wide. He shook more and Hal worried that the gun would go off whether or not the man intended it.

"Lori," Hal said. "There's someone else, someone else like you and Kaylee. Sit up."

The man's expression didn't change and Hal realized his headlights likely made it hard for the man to see. "I'm going to turn off my lights," he said.

"Don't you move!"

"I'm going to turn out my lights so you can—"

"I said don't you move! I swear to God I'll shoot you and—" The man suddenly stopped speaking and his face seemed strange for a moment, almost crumpling. His hands seemed to grow weak and Hal watched as the gun fell from them and tears welled in the man's eyes.

"My God," the man said and Hal turned to follow his gaze. Lori stood there, out of the car, pink pupils almost glowing.

***

Frank. That was what the man claimed his name was but Hal was pretty sure it was something else because he didn't respond to Frank naturally but paused as though remembering his alias whenever he was addressed. His wife was Clara, and she reacted with only the typical slowness of the infected, so Hal was pretty sure that was accurate. They hadn't stayed at the truck. It was too likely anyone passing by would stop there. Instead, they drove with Frank behind and Hal in front for about four hours until they found a private house. It was probably a farm house before, and Hal led the tiny convoy down the private road to the location. More accurately, they drove down the private road down six empty stockyards and through several hills until Frank caught a glimpse of something that appeared to be a chimney and turned to investigate. The house lay in a small valley. Of course, the house was abandoned. However, Hal found goats grazing in the backyard, shot one, and thanked God for 4H years before as he butchered it. He brought the meat inside and discovered the stove still worked, which meant the place ran on propane and not municipal gas. He set the meat to simmering and then went out back again to shoot two more goats.

Frank approached him while he was skinning them. "We can't stay together for very long," Hal said. "You make it riskier for me and I make it riskier for you. But, these goats will give us each some meat for a day or so."

"Where are you going?"

"Away." He didn't mean it as a deflection. It was the only answer he had.

"I... I heard there was somewhere we could go." The man paused. So did Hal. He looked at Frank and raised an eyebrow. "I heard there's a hospital from when it first happened, and there are still doctors there and, well, they're just past the border."

"Mexico?"

"No, Canada."

"Quebec?" The French separatists in Quebec had finally gotten their wish while the world was falling down around them. They were a separate entity. Of course, most of Canada was anarchy now. The U.S. had fallen into a structure almost like city states. Canada had done the same but not giant cities like Toronto but an endless sea of smaller settlements.

"No. What used to be British Columbia, I think. It might be on our side of the border, though."

Hal sighed. "How do you know it's not just a goose chase?"

Frank shook his head. "I don't. It probably is but what the hell else am I supposed to do?"

"I don't think we can go there together. Washington and Oregon were hit hard but they're all survivalists there, the only hope of getting through there is by being less, not more, obvious."

Frank looked hopeless, and Hal felt horrible but he added, "This is too cliché anyway. Here we are in the end of the world but there's some city of refuge our heroes can escape to? That's every goddam apocalypse movie ever made."

Surprisingly, Frank didn't back down. "Maybe you're right. Maybe it is cliché. But that might be why there's a shot. Maybe someone thought about it, set it up."

Hal sighed. "I don't think there's any hope for it but even having a destination has got to be better than what we have going on now." He was pretty sure he wouldn't be heading that direction, pretty sure Frank wasn't careful enough. The best solution was to find somewhere in the mountains, far enough from civilization that they could live without fear of discovery, somewhere with game and fresh water. Sure, the family would live like they were settlers in the 1800s but he was pretty sure they could live a fine life there until some scientist somewhere discovered a cure.

He'd been raised on a small farm, and he'd hunted year round, his father not particularly concerned with the seasons and their farm remote enough that it didn't matter. Somewhere along the way they'd procure more ammunition and some livestock, maybe some seed to get started. It would be a hard life but it would be a good life. It would be a hell of a lot better than life as it was now. He didn't want the confrontation now. Already, Frank seemed too needy. They'd develop two routes to the supposed hospital in Canada and then Hal just wouldn't show up. It was the best course of action.

Best course of action.

He felt oppressive guilt pushing down on him. Jesus. Best course of action? He looked at Frank and then stood up. "We should stick together," he said. Frank looked surprised. "It's riskier in a lot of ways but neither of us have as much of a chance alone." He paused and then added. "I don't think there's a hospital but we can find somewhere, pick up supplies along the way and start a life somewhere. We'll head that direction but let's not tell them we're heading toward a cure."

"They don't deserve hope?"

The words hurt. Hal sighed and said, "They deserve hope, hope for what's possible." He started to walk away but instead sat back down. "But they don't deserve to be disappointed again when it doesn't happen."

Frank looked like he was going to reply but then his wife stepped onto the backyard carrying a bottle. It took a moment to see what it was. Whiskey, Irish whiskey. Hal raised an eyebrow. Clearly, at the end of the world, the most important issues were food, shelter, and water. Nevertheless, he hadn't found it all that surprising that the first thing that disappeared with all the looting was the booze. The beer and wine followed shortly thereafter. You could run across a bottle of beer or wine now and again but it was all but unheard of to find the good stuff. Sure, people made homemade brews and there was always shine available but it wasn't grain based and was risky and likely laced.

Lori followed Frank's wife, and she held two cups in her hands. She handed them to Frank. Frank's wife had to adjust her plans so it took her a moment to change course and hand the bottle to Hal. He thanked her and realized he didn't know her name. "Frank," he said. "My wife's name is Lori. My daughter is Kaylee."

Frank said, "She's not my wife. I mean, she is but we never made it official. I call her my wife and she calls me her husband but I had a modest inheritance, a trust fund back in college. We would have lost the income if I were married. So... well, we never got around to making it official even though it's been... God. Why the hell didn't I just take her to the courthouse and..."

His voice trailed off and Hal took a breath. "Things aren't over, Frank. You can still marry her."

Hal watched Clara bend over toward Frank. Clara, damn it. Her name was Clara. "Clara." The woman slowly pulled away from Frank and Hal said, "I remember your name now."

It took a while for her to smile but she did. Then, she tried to speak. Hal was patient but Frank seemed embarrassed. He started to say something but Hal held up a hand. "I read somewhere that when someone stutters or has a stroke you can't finish for them. I know this isn't the same thing but maybe it feels the same way for Clara." Frank nodded and Hal quickly added, "Or for Lori or Kaylee."

Clara tried again and after an eternity got out the word *more*. Frank and Hal waited but she was done and she was smiling. Frank asked softly, "More what?"

Lori answered. "Bar," she said. "Whole bar." Hal thought she spoke more quickly than she had in a while and he smiled broadly. She smiled back. Clara smiled as well. They seemed proud about their discovery, and Hal wondered at a world thrown back a hundred years or more where nonetheless, the discovery of spirits was a fabulous thing.

He smiled at the two of them. "Do you two want to get glasses?" Lori looked surprised and he said, "I think it will be fine. No interactions with the drugs and alcohol isn't going to spread any infection." He smiled again. "Just one glass, though." Lori took Clara's hand. He watched them slowly walk away and found it strange they could move with excitement but still move so slowly.

"You think it's an infection, then?"

Hal shrugged. "I think I want my wife to feel normal." He finished skinning the second goat and said, "Can you see if there's a shovel or something? We should bury the skins and the entrails. Just in case there are any of them around."

Frank nodded and stood. By the time he returned, the wives were back with glasses. Hal stood and said, "Frank and I need to clean up. How about you pour the drinks." He purposely didn't open the bottle and took Frank a short distance away, dragging the skins and the entrails atop them with him. Frank dug and Hal said, "Lori likes to do things even if it takes a long time. I think she's getting faster, too."

"She's getting better?"

Hal nodded. "Yeah, I think so. Use it or lose it, maybe."

***

By the time they finished with the two new skins and the one from earlier, the women had glasses full and waiting. Everyone also had a plate of stewed goat and Kaylee ate inside. Hal sat next to Lori and kissed her cheek. Frank seemed surprised but he leaned over and kissed Clara as well. Hal saw movement and panic welled up for a moment but it was Kaylee, stepping closer and then making her slow way to Hal and Lori. He kissed her cheek as well and said, "It's time for bed, little one." She groaned but then simply lay at his feet and closed her eyes. He smiled and shrugged and then took a sip of his whiskey.

Heaven.

Jesus. How long had it been? He drank bourbon, sometimes Tennessee, but he didn't like Irish whiskey. It just didn't go down as smoothly as bourbon. Hate was probably too strong a term but he'd skipped the hard stuff altogether if his preference wasn't available.

But it tasted like Heaven nonetheless. It burned nicely going down and he savored it but then noticed the carcasses of the goats on the porch. "We'll have to limit it to one drink until we can get those processed. I think we might have to smoke them."

Lori touched his hand and he turned his head. She took a long time to form words but she finally managed to say, "RV."

Hal nodded and said, "We don't have it anymore, Honey. We..." He trailed off because he was almost... it sure as hell seemed like she rolled her eyes. She smiled a half smile, a smile closer to one of her sardonic smiles from before. He suddenly wanted her again and he breathed in sharply. He fought back the emotions, though, and said. "Here. You mean there's an RV here." She nodded slowly. "Where?"

She shrugged. It took a long time to figure out exactly what expression she tried to make but she shrugged. "Did you see an RV?" Hal asked.

Her response came slowly but she said, "Clara."

Frank turned to Clara. "Did you see an RV?"

Clara shook her head slowly and then said, "Come, follow...Nathan."

Nathan. Frank was Nathan. Hal smiled but didn't say anything. Frank looked ashamed and then said, "Nathan is my middle name. What did she mean?"

Hal said, "Ask her. She's still Clara, Nathan."

He turned to his wife. "What do you mean?"

Clara stood and motioned for him to follow. Frank stood and so did Hal. Lori smiled and said, "Kaylee." She didn't stand. Hal nodded and kissed her cheek. Clara turned around and began her slow walk back into the house. She led them through the kitchen and into a small adjoining room. The adjoining room had the bar, a beautiful oak bar someone sank a great deal of money into. He paused and looked behind it. Mostly glassware but five more bottles of Irish whiskey were in an open box. He saw a few mixers, a bottle of gin, and a half-open bottle of vodka.

He put the gin in the empty slot in the case of whiskey and lifted it to the top of the bar. Lori stared disapprovingly at him, and he was almost too shocked by her ability to create the expression to protest. "Alcohol is antiseptic," he said. "We may drink a little bit for special occasions but this is for medicine." He was almost certain she rolled her eyes again but she did it with a smile. He sighed. "Clara, please show me the RV."

He followed slowly behind the women as Clara walked to a door, opened it, and then stepped out of the way. She took a great deal of time to gesture for him to look inside but he waited patiently. Lori was very far advanced compared to Clara. Perhaps Clara was simply advanced in the disease. He didn't know. He nodded to her and stepped inside the room.

It was a pantry, and it was remarkable because the pantry was full. There were canned goods as well as pasta and beans in canisters embossed with roses and grapes. There was even hot chocolate in a tin, and he wondered why nobody had looted the house. In fact, the house seemed pretty damned intact altogether, and that made no sense at all. He turned back to Clara and said, "This is good, really good. Why did you say RV, though?"

She lifted her hand and Hal realized she was pointing. He'd grown accustomed to waiting for Lori or Kaylee to finish their words and gestures so the impatience that hit him suddenly was unexpected. He held on even though he had to clench his teeth to do so and when she stopped moving her hand he looked where she pointed. On the top shelf were RV supplies. There were cans of toilet treatment, rolls of tissue designed for portable toilets, and a few other odds and ends. There were also batteries, large batteries he assumed handled the RV auxiliary power. Clara hadn't seen an RV. She'd seen evidence of one. That was inductive reasoning. That was remarkable.

He turned. "This is a great discovery. The RV might be here and we'll have to search the property. On the other hand, the people who lived here might have been traveling when... well, when everything happened." Both women nodded and he made it official. Lori only took about two-thirds of the time to complete the affirmation as Clara took. He smiled and said, "Why don't we finish our drinks and in the morning we can try to find the RV?"

She nodded, and Hal thought perhaps she nodded more quickly than she had before.

***

He made love to Lori again, this time in a king sized bed under dusty blankets but blankets still. He felt normal, and though he thought perhaps it was better because they'd broken the ice by the truck he suspected it was more than that. She was better. She'd been awkward before, physically awkward. She didn't move like some kind of porn star now but she moved a hell of a lot faster than she had before. By the truck, she was like a virgin experiencing things for the first awkward time. Now, she was like a 1970s European soft core actress, moving slowly and gently but still actively participating. He held tightly to her afterward and then rolled over and she put one leg over him and her head on his shoulder.

Like before.

Like before everything.

He stroked her back and realized she was crying softly. He lifted her head and kissed her. "We're going to get through this," he said. "We will." She kissed him, on his mouth, and though it still took a while, she told him she loved him.

She rolled off and though she was slow, she was still faster than before. He was certain of it. He watched her walk to the walk-in closet and open it. Kaylee lay there sleeping. Was it activity that did it? Was it like physical therapy? Maybe they could never get rid of the pink eyes but was it really something as simple as using it or losing it? He chuckled softly and Lori turned to look at him. He didn't tell her he was considering marathon sex sessions as treatment. Instead, he told her he loved her and he was happy and that someday they would find a house like this where they could try to be normal. She smiled and came back to bed.

In the morning, he was surprised to find Clara up and excited. Frank/Nathan was still asleep. Lori walked to Clara and hugged her, and Hal wondered if there was some kind of secret language the two shared. Did all of the infected share a language? He wondered why they didn't attack each other, the ones who were far gone with the condition. He'd always assumed there was something in the disease, some pheromone or something. With the way the two interacted, though, he thought perhaps there was more. Finally, Lori let go and walked to Hank. Her expressions were definitely clearer. Were they? Was he too hopeful?

She kissed him and said, "She found it." He waited but that was it. She'd said the words and there was almost no delay. She seemed like she was on the brink of laughing at his shocked expression and she kissed him again. Her second sentence took much longer to get out. "Hurry before her boss wakes up."

He nodded and started toward Clara but then stopped. "Boss?"

Clara looked a little embarrassed but from behind him, Lori giggled and it actually almost sounded like a giggle. He turned to look at her and the smile that greeted him was almost mischievous.

***

The RV was a class C. They'd rented one every summer before Kaylee and then one week a year. This was a newer model. It was in something that looked like a barn, and it was hooked up, still plugged in and still connected to the sewer drain. Hal tried the driver's door. It worked. The keys hung from the visor. He recognized the ignition keys but he also recognized the keys to all of the compartments along the side as well as the side door. He grabbed them and walked around. The side door was unlocked so he didn't have to use the key. When he opened the door, a step slid out with an electric whirring sound. There was still power. He stepped inside. The thing was clean. Perfectly clean.

Except for the dust.

There weren't any cobwebs but he could smell cedar and mothballs. He imagined the owners were in their fifties before everything fell apart. He imagined the husband was an engineer or something, someone who worked off checklists. Even the dust wasn't that bad. He surveyed things. The stove was propane rather than electric. That was good. There was a bunk above the cab. A couch. It became a bed. The dining area sat four or five and it collapsed into a bed as well. He walked past the refrigerator and saw the shower and the bathroom. Good working order, it appeared. He opened the door beyond them and stared in at the master room. Again, it was very well kept. Only dust.

Hall walked back out and tested the engine. Worked. He went back outside and opened each compartment in turn. The RV was stocked will all of the RV essentials. Flares, tool kit, first aid kit, spare bulbs, spare fuses. He was particularly happy to find a solar switch right next to the propane tanks. He climbed underneath. The propane tank was detachable. That was good. It was still fairly common to come across standard propane tanks with gas. It was near to impossible to find anywhere to fill them. He climbed into the driver's seat and turned the key. He didn't know why he found it so surprising that the RV worked but it worked. He saw there were two tanks and saw the thing ran on diesel. That would actually make things easier. There were far more abandoned trucks than cars. The gauge showed a full tank. He flipped a switch above it and the gauge fell to two-thirds of a tank. Two tanks. Good to know.

He turned off the engine and said, "Your boss?"

Clara looked embarrassed again and Hal realized she was probably twenty years younger than Frank. "Are you safe with him?" She nodded her head vigorously or at least as vigorously as she could and Hal nodded. "Okay. We have some work to do. Why don't you two and Kaylee see about cleaning this up and then packing up the food and the supplies. He thought a moment and then said, "Hold on." He drove forward and out of the barn. He turned off the engine again and then climbed out. He walked several yards away and caught the glint of panels on the roof. He made his way back, opened the compartment, and toggled the switch that initiated the solar power. Then, he climbed back into the RV and held his breath as he reached for a light switch.

It worked.

He sat down on the couch and tried to figure out how to handle things. He sure as hell wasn't going to let Frank or Nathan or whatever the hell his name was drive the RV but that meant leaving his car behind and he wasn't inclined to give up his car. It was a stupid vanity, sure, but it was still there. He sighed and considered just taking Lori and Kaylee and leaving. He wanted to take Clara, too, imagined what it had to be like. The girl was probably in her very early twenties. She was probably eighteen or nineteen before she became infected, and that meant the asshole had been fucking a girl who was all but a child.

Jesus. Was he just keeping her around for the guaranteed lay?

He felt bile rising in his throat and leapt from the couch and out of the RV, retching horribly as he shot partially digested goat onto the grass. He stumbled farther away from the RV and that was when he saw the glint of metal against the side of the barn. He made his way over and then stopped a few yards away. There were two of them, obviously the owners of the RV. They screamed when they saw him and stretched their hands toward him but they were pinned down. Their throats had deteriorated enough that their screams were no more than raspy whispers.

He stepped closer. It was hard to see exactly what had fallen on them but it looked like machined steel. A closer look told him it was almost like part of the frame of a pre-fabricated steel building. They were four or five yards from the side of the barn. He looked up. There were more of the steel frames on the roof of the barn. He still couldn't see how it had worked to pin them but thought perhaps they'd climbed on the roof or something like that and fallen...no. It didn't make sense. They were too old to climb. More likely an animal climbed on the roof at the wrong moment and a poorly balanced stack shifted.

They were pinned opposite each other, and that made the situation even more tragic. Each had torn the flesh from the others legs. A goat skeleton lay next to the man as well. Hal sighed and reached for his gun.

Damn.

He made his way back toward the house and into the bedroom where he'd slept. He reached for the duffel bag but stopped when he saw movement. "I'm sorry," Frank/Nathan said. "But I'm taking the RV. I'm taking it with Clara." Hal turned his head slowly. The man had Hal's gun.

"Does Clara know about this?"

"Wake up. Clara doesn't know anything. None of them do." The man gestured with the gun. Hal wasn't sure if he knew how to use it but the man seemed comfortable with it in his hand. "We're with walking vegetables. That's it. They're good for pussy and nothing else." He paused and his smile almost made Hal sick again. "Good pussy, though. The best. They spread their legs when you tell them to and they don't argue with you afterward. You know, Clara was a huge problem before all this happened. Now she knows her place."

"Was she going to tell your wife, Frank?"

The man's eyes narrowed. Hal knew he'd hit a nerve but the man replied evenly. "Right now, you and your pets get to live. We'll take the RV and the supplies and we'll leave. You want to change that? You want me to put a bullet in your brain and have more than one pair of docile legs to spread whenever I want?"

His instinct was to leap up and attack but Hal fought down the urge. Then, he saw Clara in the doorway. He took a deep breath. "Don't you love Clara?"

The man laughed. "Love? That was all she wanted before this shit happened. Look, I loved the way she could move her body, I'll give you that. I loved that I could do anything, anything at all. If my wife didn't give it to me, Clara would. Sure, she's more like some fucking plastic blow up doll now but that's better than nothing."

"Don't you give a damn about how she feels?"

"How she feels? Grow up. Jesus. Listen up, Boy Scout. I really care about how she feels when I'm screwing her. How's that?" Clara's eyes were sad, not quite filled with tears but sad. Hal watched her step away and to cover the noise he stood up. Immediately, Frank trained the gun on him and said, "What the hell do you think you're doing?"

Hal lifted his hands. "I want to go downstairs and get you keys so you can leave." He wanted to add how much Frank sickened him but he didn't. "Unless you want to try them yourself," he said.

Frank eyed him narrowly and said, "Okay. Let's go." Hal walked carefully past him and out of the bedroom. The man walked behind him, making his steps obvious, making sure Hal knew he was there.

"Is it Frank or is it Nathan?"

"What?"

"Your real name. Which is it?"

"Why the hell does that matter anymore?"

Hal shrugged. It didn't matter, not really. "Were you in love with your wife before this happened?"

"You talk too much."

"What if they can still think? What if they can still feel?" It was a pretty damned stupid question, really. The man didn't give a damn about her thoughts and her feelings before.

"Have you ever had an affair?"

"No."

There was a pause. They were near the door to the backyard now, and Hal could almost see the expression on Frank's face in the glass door. It was indecision. "You know," Hal began but the man interrupted him.

"When you're married your wife has expectations all the time. Then some beautiful young girl shows up at your office and she adores you, she wants you without all those expectations. You don't have to prove anything to her. You don't have to be anything than older and her boss for her to love everything about you."

Hal reached the door. "It's not too late to give her a real reason to love you."

"Just get the keys, and don't try anything."

Hal slid the door open and stepped out. He walked to the RV, moving slowly in the hopes a brilliant plan would spring to mind but nothing came. He could take Frank, Nathan. He could take whatever the hell his name was but he wasn't sure he could do it without a wound and he wasn't confident he could keep that wound from pushing him into sepsis. "Listen. This is a bad choice—"

"Just shut up! This is happening and you can either live with it or die right here."

He sighed again and made walked to the driver side door. He opened it and pulled down the visor. The keys were gone. "You already took the keys?"

"What? What the hell are you talking about?"

He turned to face him. "What kind of game are you playing? The keys are already gone."

Frank looked nervous, frightened. "I may not be the kind of guy who stars in blockbusters but I have the goddam gun and I'll use it." Hal wasn't certain if he'd really use it but he was certain the man had no morality left.

"I don't have them. They're gone."

"I will kill your daughter and then your—"

"Hid... them..." Hal turned to see Clara. She had her arm up and pointed at Hal. She repeated the words and an eternity passed as she did. Lori and Kaylee stood next to her, looking scared.

Frank/Nathan smiled and walked toward them. "You're going to tell me where you hid the damned keys or you can just say goodbye to one of them. Which one Hal? You want to say goodbye to your already dead wife or your already dead daughter?" He shouted the last words and raised the gun. Hal prepared to leap toward him as his heart raced but Clara stepped in front of her ex-boss.

"You...don't...love...me?"

Frank lifted up his hands. "Of course I do," he said sweetly. "I'm doing all of this for you."

"Heard... talk... him."

"Darling," he said. "Anything you heard I only said because he's dangerous. That's why I need the keys, to get away from him." He lifted his arm and pointed the gun at Kaylee. "You have three seconds, Hal." Hal prepared to attack but Clara put her hand on Frank's wrist.

"I... know... hid... them..."

Frank smiled and the smile grew malicious as he turned to Hal and said, "See. She knows her place." He gestured with the gun and Hal followed the direction until he stood next to Lori and Kaylee. Frank turned his attention back to Clara. "Where did you see him hide them?"

"No... I... hid..."

Something was wrong. Hal didn't know what it was but Lori wasn't afraid. She was sad. He was pretty sure she was sad. It was possible he misinterpreted her expression but he didn't think so. He'd seen that expression time and time again. Lori wasn't afraid.

Kaylee was.

Kaylee was afraid. She held tightly to Lori's hand and stared at her father expectantly. She expected something from him, something miraculous. Hal wondered for a moment why he still found it so difficult to accept his daughter's disappointment, even now when life itself was nothing but disappointment. He sighed and said, "You can still stop this, Frank."

"You don't know anything," the man said. "My name isn't Nathan or Frank. That was my company."

"Frank and Nathan's? The video stores?" Hal tried to remember the press releases. The places would be out of business but they kept their adult choices long after the larger chains bowed to pressure. Then, abruptly, the firm announced some kind of accounting problems. Hal shook his head. "The infection was the only thing that kept you out of prison."

"Like this isn't prison?" The man's eyes narrowed. "Now give me the keys."

"I don't know where they are."

"I... know..."

The man nodded. "Get something to tie him to the RV." Clara looked around in confusion and the man snapped, "Rope damn it. Get some God damned rope or something." The girl jumped (as much as someone in her condition could) and then went to the RV, opening one of the side compartments and rummaging around. That just didn't make sense.

Didn't make sense?

That was bullshit.

She wouldn't have thought to look there. What the hell was going on? He turned to look at Clara but couldn't see anything of note. He turned to look at Lori. She still looked sad but there was definitely no fear. Clara stood up.

Christ.

She had a gun, a shotgun. It wasn't one of Hal's, and Hal hadn't seen it with Frank/Nathan's things. It wasn't too surprising that there'd be a gun on property in this part of the country or really in any part of the country in a home so secluded but it was surprising Clara found it instead of Hal.

"Not..." Clara began as she pointed the gun at Frank/Nathan. "Not..."

"Steal," Lori said.

Clara nodded slowly. "Yes. Not steal RV."

Frank looked incredulous and Hal understood. Were they getting better or were they always better? Were their minds just stiff, needing stretching? It was impossible. None of it made sense.

Except the guns.

They made far too much sense.

Frank/Nathan's face remained incredulous for a moment and Hal looked back at Clara. He doubted she'd ever used a gun in real life. He knew Lori hadn't. The shotgun was a pump shotgun and from the state of the RV, Hal doubted the man who'd owned it was the type to leave a shell in the chamber. He looked back at Frank and watched his face grow angry. The man trained the gun on Clara, murder evident in his expression.

"Wait," Hal said softly. "I know where the keys are."

"No!" He turned to look at Lori. She hadn't managed that level of intensity in her voice for a very long time.

"Where are they?"

"I'll show you," Hal said.

He wasn't certain what the hell he was going. All he knew for certain was that if the situation remained as it was Frank would fire and it was likely Clara would die. It might be too much of a stretch for Frank to accept that Lori and Clara had collaborated on the little insurrection but the risk was too high. He had to get the man to follow him and somehow find an opportunity to get the gun away from him.

He'd have to kill him.

Hal felt horrible about it but there wasn't any choice. He had to kill him. The man would always be a threat and he'd be a greater threat in close quarters. He turned to Clara. "Lower the gun, Clara."

"No." He thought for a moment her eyes glinted with tears.

"Please, Clara," he said. "It will be okay. We'll all be okay." It seemed to take forever but the barrel of the shotgun finally came down.

"Show me," Frank said. Hal walked around the front of the RV with no real idea where he planned to go and caught movement in the distance. He paused and stared. There were dozens of them. Maybe tens of dozens. "What the hell are those?" Frank asked.

"Goats," Hal said.

"Then why the hell is there grass? That many goats would have decimated this place. It should be dirt."

Hal shrugged. It was a good question. There was no reason for the goats to leave... Hal sighed. "The keys are this way," he said as he walked into the grass and then turned toward the barn. He walked and counted the steps. Frank spoke about five steps sooner than he'd expected him to.

"Wait!" Hal stopped and turned. Frank looked at him narrowly. "You think you're so damned smart, don't you. You have a gun stashed? Hung the keys up next to keys? You want the harem to yourself, you asshole?"

Hall shook his head sadly. "There's no gun."

"Bullshit. Where are the keys?" Hal sighed, shook his head sadly one more time, turned and pointed. Frank smirked slightly and said, "Okay.

You move toward the left for me. I'm going to walk ahead but this gun will be on you the whole time. Don't get any ideas or I won't just take the damned RV. I'll put a god damned bullet in your head and leave you right where it's parked."

Hal didn't reply. He sighed and stepped to the left and then watched as the man stepped next to him, moving at a slight angle so the gun remained trained on Hal's body. Now was the time. A quick strike with his leg to the knee would incapacitate him, and if he got a shot off it would go wide, very wide. Nothing about the man was physically imposing. A quick kick and a quick follow up with his fist would incapacitate him, eliminate the threat, and diffuse the entire situation. The kick would take less than a second.

He didn't kick him. Instead, he walked along sadly. "There's still time to stop all this," he said softly. Frank stopped and turned fully toward him. There was just a little bit of uncertainty in his eyes. That was enough. A quick fist to his throat would incapacitate him with no real damage. A simple motion, really. A step forward, putting his weight on his right leg and a straight jab to ensure he hit the throat and not the side of the next. Frank would probably drop the gun but it wouldn't matter if he didn't. He'd be useless. He'd be utterly useless.

Hal desperately wanted to jab at his throat. All morality suggested he should but he didn't. Frank walked backward, the gun trained on Hal and he scowled. "You'd like that, right? We all go our merry way and I spend every second wondering when you're going to shoot me in the back of the head. That's what this is all about, you just waiting for the chance. You're lucky I don't just kill you. It's mercy to let you live. You'd never do it for me." Hal stopped moving. Frank stopped as well but then smiled. "Don't you dare try anything." He kept the gun trained on Hal before he turned around.

Before he turned around and screamed.

Before he turned around and the female put her teeth into his calf and tore a chunk of it out. The gun fell to the ground and bounced slightly. Hal felt a wave of guilt as Frank lunged for it, succeeding only in falling to the ground and making it possible for the male to get to his arm as the man screamed and flailed about impotently. Frank screamed primal screams, wordless screams.

Panicked screams.

Hal might have been able to save him before the male got involved. He couldn't now. He couldn't even offer him a release from the pain. The gun was too close to the two infected. He wanted to shoot him, to give him that mercy but the gun was too close. He stared, though he desperately wanted to look away. He stared and considered it penance that he should watch a man eaten alive, a man murdered by Hal.

Murder?

Self-defense?

There was no rationalizing it, as much as he wanted to. He'd consciously decided to kill him, consciously decided to do so with the husband and wife zombies who themselves deserved the mercy of permanent darkness. He looked at Frank. The man beat at the male eating his arm but he couldn't have much strength left. Anything he gained from adrenaline was counteracted by the loss of blood. Already, the woman had a large portion of his calf stripped from the bone so that sickly white mingled with the red and black gore.

He could chance the gun. He could move in, grab it, back off, and put a bullet in Frank's head. Perhaps that would be the only thing that allowed him to sleep soundly ever again. It was too close. The male might be distracted by his meal but Hal couldn't risk it. If he were killed, or even hurt, the chances for Lori and Kaylee grew slight and that wasn't acceptable. There was no choice but to—

His ears seemed to explode with pain as he watched Frank's head disappear into red vapor. He turned, a little deaf, and saw Clara holding the shotgun. He wasn't certain if he'd ever experienced such profound gratitude and profound guilt at the same time. Surprise, too. She'd known how to chamber a round, perhaps even how to load the gun.

Frank didn't scream anymore but the meal continued and he held out his hand. Clara seemed relieved to give him the weapon. He trained it on the male and then the female, awarding peace to the two of them but still leaving images in his head he knew would linger. He looked at Clara. Her expression was unreadable.

"Sorry," she said. Hal didn't know if she said it to apologize to him or to Frank.

"I'll bury him," he said.

She nodded and said, "Them... too."

"Yes," he said. "Can you, can you go back to the RV? Can you make sure Lori and Kaylee know you're fine, know I'm fine?" She nodded again and seemed grateful for a purpose as she walked away. Hal leaned against the side of the barn and slowly slid to a seated position, holding his head in his hands.

***

"Why don't we stay?" It was early, and Hal opened his eyes to see Lori staring back at him. She seemed normal again, normal but for the pink pupils. She seemed normal and he was certain there'd been no hesitation in her voice.

"What did you say?"

"Why don't we stay?" He sat up and stared at her. The bodies were buried and buried deeply. He'd done it unnecessarily, really. He'd dug deep for his own benefit, to make the task somehow more meaningful, more profound. He hadn't done it to keep the bodies from attracting other infected but it would have the same effect nonetheless. He'd finished and somehow leaving didn't make sense and they all ended up remaining for one more night.

One more.

"What if he was right, Lori?" he asked. "What if there's a place in Canada where they're trying to find a cure. What if there's a safe haven."

"He was a liar." Again, her voice came so naturally, so perfectly that he felt a flood of sudden and desperate desire for her. He reached for her and pulled her to him, kissing her deeply. They made love, and this time without the almost overwhelming urgency they'd shared at the side of the road by the truck. Instead, he explored her slowly and wept when they finished so she held him and stroked his hair as he faded to sleep again. He awoke to the smell of coffee. He'd need to start rationing things.

He made his way down and to the kitchen. Lori sat at the table and smiled at him. "Why don't we stay?" she asked again as she got up and walked to the coffee pot. She poured him a mug and handed it to him. "Why don't we stay?"

He looked out the sliding glass window and saw Clara playing with Kaylee. Even happy, Kaylee always had a haunted look but it didn't seem to be there at the moment. Surely it was his eyes and not her expression but he didn't mind. "What if there's a haven out there?"

"Here is a haven."

He smiled but kept his eyes on Kaylee. "Is Clara okay?"

She didn't reply so he turned to look at her. "Here is a haven," she repeated.

It was secluded. There were goats that would last for some time, perpetually if he managed the stock and bred them. He could probably get a garden working. They could always leave later. They could keep the RV stocked and ready to go at a moment's notice. On the other hand, they could likely gather others to the place.

"Here is a haven," she said insistently.

"I suppose it is," he said. Lori reached over and put her hand over his, squeezing gently.

<u>CLICK HERE FOR BOOK TWO OF "DEAD BODIES BITE"</u> [1]

---

1.   http://www.pochepictures.com/deadbodiesbite.html